Chapter Titles

Chapter 1 Whispers of Change

Chapter 2 A Storm on the Horizon

Chapter 3 Embracing the Everyday

Chapter 4 - Future thoughts

Chapter 5 Awakening the Ordinary

Chapter 6 Finding Clarity in the Chaos

Chapter 7 A Journey of Self-Discover

Chapter 8 Uncovering New Beginnings

Chapter 9 The Spark of Change

Chapter 10 Breaking the Cycle

Chapter 11 Awakening to Possibility

Chapter 12 A Glimpse of Tomorrow

Chapter 13 The Unknown

Chapter 14 A New Dawn

Chapter 1

Whispers of Change

On a warm, sun-drenched Sunday evening, Jasmine reclined on her plush, cream-colored lounger, beautifully integrated into her meticulously designed garden that boasted a symphony of vibrant flowers and dense greenery.

Cradling a glass of perfectly chilled prosecco, the liquid shimmered like liquid diamonds in the amber light of the fading sun. Her bare feet, soft against the fabric of the lounger, savored the gentle warmth radiating from the earth beneath, a tranquil contrast to the responsibilities that awaited her in the coming week.

The newly planted trees, their leaves a vibrant emerald, swayed gracefully in the mild evening breeze, their movement creating a mesmerizing dance that served as a serene backdrop to her thoughts. She closed her eyes, allowing the soft sounds of nature—the distant chirping of crickets and the rustle of leaves—to wash over her. In her mind, she longed for that cherished hour—5 PM on Friday—when the weight of her weekly responsibilities would finally begin to lift, heralding the arrival of a brief escape from the routines that often consumed her days.

As the shadow of Monday loomed ominously, like an unwelcome guest threatening to ruin her peaceful retreat, she sank deeper into the cushioned embrace of her lounger.

Each passing minute boosted her desire to extend the bliss of the weekend, cherishing the vibrant hues of her garden—a mix of vibrant color with pink peonies, bright yellow daisies, and delicate lavender wafting their sweet fragrance through the air, reminding her of life's exquisite beauty even as the clock edged closer to 11 PM.

With a soft sigh laced with wistfulness, Jasmine reluctantly sat up from her cozy haven. She placed her nearly empty glass—a delicate flute that had once sparkled with enthusiasm—on the polished walnut dining room table, its rich finish glistening in the dim light. With a casual flick of her wrist, she tossed the now-empty prosecco bottle into the recycling bin, its contents fading into a distant memory, much like the enchanting weekend itself.

After taking a moment to secure her sanctuary, ensuring the doors were locked tight against the encroaching night, walked up the staircase, each step creaking softly in the silence. Thoughts of her garden lingered in her mind; the image of those trees swaying in the gentle breeze remained with her like a tranquil, almost magical spell as she sought to ease into her evening routine, preparing for the oncoming embrace of sleep.

As she settled beneath soft, inviting layers of her cozy quilt, woven with threads of deep indigo and silver, a wave of tranquility washed over her, wrapping her in a comforting cocoon. Yet, just as she began to drift into a peaceful slumber, a sudden flash of lightning sliced through the darkening sky, bright and electric. Its bold glow illuminated her room for a brief moment, casting frightening shadows that moved wildly on the walls of her bedroom.

Almost immediately filling the silence, the air vibrated with the low, rumbling growl of thunder—a deep resonance echoing through the atmosphere, echoing around the sky's and preparing for an impending storm. It felt as though the sky was communicating a message, one soaked with significance.

"Well, it has been an exceptionally warm weekend," she murmured to herself, a hint of unease creeping into her thoughts as the air grew heavier, thick with the promise of the impending storm.

Little did Jasmine know, this sudden shift in weather was not merely a random occurrence, but a powerful profound change in her life—one that she would soon come to realize was far more significant than she could ever have anticipated.

Chapter 2

A Storm on the Horizon

Days unfolded into an elaborate cycle, each melding into the next, marking yet another Monday that promised new beginnings. The familiar sound of her alarm clock blared at precisely 5:50 AM, its shrill tone piercing through Jasmine's slumber and gently nudging her into her morning routine.

Sleep-laden eyes, she stumbled into her cozy kitchen, where the rich aroma of freshly brewed coffee enveloped her like a warm embrace, a comforting reminder of the power found in daily rituals. The sunlight streamed through the small window, casting a golden hue across the countertops and illuminating the faded photographs that adorned the walls—moments frozen in time.

As she moved through her morning routine—pouring steaming coffee into her beloved, chipped ceramic mug, lacing up her sturdy, well-worn sneakers, and navigating the bustling streets filled with familiar faces—each element of her world felt transformed.

As she drove to work, she barely noticed where she was going; every morning seemed the same, almost like a choreographed movie scene. Each stoplight became a moment to breathe, allowing her a brief pause to gather her thoughts, while the honks from impatient drivers served as reminders of her resilience.

Once bursting with ambition and dreams of grandeur, Jasmine was awakening to the potential of her now, recognizing the beauty in embracing the familiar, the details of which had begun to fade into background noise. Each time she turned the key in her apartment door, the creak of the worn hinges resonated like an invitation to reflect on her growth, serving as a poignant reminder of her strength and endurance through challenges.

Yet beneath the surface, frustration simmered within her a constant hum punctuating her everyday life, signaling a call to action as she confronted the absurdity of her situation. The dull anticipation of the weekend, which once promised a much-needed break from her routine, had shifted into a catalyst for change each tick of the clock heralding an opportunity to seize the moment and reshape her narrative. The vibrancy of life she had once celebrated began to awaken within her, rekindled by her courage to actively seek transformation.

In a determined effort to break free from this mundane cycle, Jasmine committed herself to discovering a path forward. She began to meticulously track her days in a worn notebook, its pages yellowed with age and filled with inked reflections, capturing even the smallest details to uncover insights that might guide her.

The act of writing became a powerful outlet for her very mixed emotions, with ink on paper transforming her frustration into clarity and hope, offering a clearer lens through which to view her life.

This journey, while fraught with challenges, sparked a flicker of motivation that illuminated her path. Armed with her notebook and an unwavering curiosity, she set out to understand the essence of her journey, diving deep into her own thoughts and feelings.

With each entry, she reclaimed the excitement and spontaneity that once defined her vibrant life, resolute in her quest to navigate beyond the fog and fully embrace the kaleidoscopic world that awaited her.

Chapter 3

Embracing the Everyday

She pulled the key from the ignition, enjoying a fleeting moment of silence before bracing herself for the reality of her grueling 12-hour shift.

Taking a deep breath, she swung open the café door, where the scent of freshly ground coffee beans welcomed her like a warm hug, instantly bringing her spirits to a level she could greet customers with.

As she got behind the counter and put her apron on, she greeted her colleagues Tom and Sarah with an over-rehearsed, "How are you all on this AMAZING day?"

"Oh, we're just surviving, you know," Tom replied, rolling his eyes with a smirk. "I've already dealt with two customers who came to the counter. When I didn't serve them quickly enough, one of them shouted, 'I ordered it on the app, so if I can do your job quickly, why can't you?'"

"Only two? Clearly, you haven't had the true experience of the morning shift yet," Jasmine teased. "You have worked the mid-shift too much," she said, leaning against the counter and giggling. "Have you met our dear Mrs. Smith?"

Tom shook his head. Sarah chuckled. "Oh, don't remind me! I'm still recovering from yesterday's 'espresso with a sprinkle of cinnamon' debacle. She nearly threw her drink at me!"

Just then, the unmistakable jingling of the doorbell signaled the arrival of Mrs. Smith, a very particular regular whose expectations soared higher than the heavens.

Today, her random request was a tall caramel latte with vanilla and a sprinkle of paprika, all topped with creamy oat milk. This caused Jasmine and anyone in earshot to raise her eyebrow.

"Good morning, Mrs. Smith! What can we do for you today?" Jasmine asked, her cheerfulness barely masking her skepticism.

Mrs. Smith peered over her reading glasses, pursing her lips. "I want my usual, but can you make sure to add a dash of paprika? It's vital for flavor!" "Paprika? Right..." Jasmine looked over at Sarah, who was desperately holding back laughter. "Sure, one paprika latte coming right up!"

"No dear, a caramel latte. Can't you get that right?" Mrs. Smith barked back.

As she reluctantly turned her back on the demanding customer, she rolled her eyes and muttered under her breath, "The customer is always right... until they're wrong."

Moments later, as she handed over the concoction, Mrs. Smith took a tentative sip, her face changing into instant outrage. "This is wrong! It's normal milk, not oat!" she declared so the whole café could hear.

"Actually, it's oat milk, Mrs. Smith," Sarah stepped in quickly and held up the carton clearly labeled "oat milk."

Mrs. Smith remained unyielding, retorting, "You've swapped the milk. You're just trying to pull the wool over my eyes! I demand perfection! You understand?"

Jasmine, channeling her best customer service persona, forced a smile, "Mrs. Smith, I assure you, we would never do that. You're our favorite customer!"

"Well, I'd prefer to be treated like one!" Mrs. Smith huffed as she stormed away.

As the door swung shut behind her, Tom peeked his head around the storeroom door, shaking his head with a grin. "Jaz, you're going to get yourself in trouble one of these days."

Jasmine shrugged with a playful smirk. "Oh, I thrive on chaos. Just wait until the lunch rush. Who knows what other delights today will bring?"

"Just don't let them put paprika in anything else!" Sarah added, stifling her laughter.

"Consider it done! Now, who's next?" Jasmine called out, ready for whatever the day had in store.

Chapter 4

Future Thoughts

On a warm, sunny Sunday evening, Jasmine reclined on her plush, cream-colored sun lounger, meticulously positioned beneath the shade of a sprawling oak tree in her beautifully designed garden. The sun dipped low on the horizon, casting a golden hue over her carefully curated flowerbeds filled with vibrant daisies and roses.

Cradling a crystal glass filled with perfectly chilled prosecco, she watched as the spirited bubbles danced in the glass, sparkling in the fading sunlight.

Her bare feet, decorated with a fresh coat of coral nail polish that gleamed in the waning light, rested comfortably on the cushioned footrest, while the gentle warmth of the sun seeped into her skin. Jasmine's garden was a sanctuary of serenity, with newly planted trees swaying gently in the soft, welcome breeze.

Their green leaves rustled softly, sharing secrets with one another, as they blended with the sweet fragrance of the nearby lavender bushes in full bloom, their purple spikes gently swaying.

Closing her eyes, Jasmine allowed her mind to drift, reveling in that perfect hour—5 PM on Friday—when the everyday responsibilities of the week fell away, leaving behind only promises of weekend bliss. But as the looming shadow of Monday sank heavily onto her shoulders, she sank deeper into her lounge chair, desperate to steal just a little more time from the magical tranquility of Sunday before it faded into laborious routine once more.

As the clock approached 11 PM, a gentle wave of sleepiness washed over her like a soft tide, nudging her to acknowledge the inevitable end of the weekend. With a soft sigh of resignation, she reluctantly rose from the comfort of her seat, her dreams of extended relaxation scattering like morning fog. Setting her glass down on the polished oak dining table, she placed the now-empty prosecco bottle into the recycling bin, its bubbly spirit fading into a distant memory.

After performing a final check that her home—her cherished sanctuary—was securely locked, she made her way upstairs, each step echoing the stillness of her earlier calm. Thoughts flitted through her mind like restless butterflies, imagining potential enhancements for her garden—visions of vibrant petunias, sun-drenched cozy seating areas, and enchanting fairy lights making the space stunning after dark, even though the time for action felt disturbingly far away.

As she snuggled under the soft, cozy blankets of her bed, the serene silence was abruptly shattered by a sudden flash of lightning that illuminated her room. Almost immediately, a low rumble of thunder rolled through the atmosphere, its deep resonance echoing like a distant drumbeat, steadily growing in intensity with each passing moment.

"Well, it has been an exceptionally warm weekend," she muttered to herself, a thread of unease weaving through her thoughts as she sensed the air thickening with the impending storm. The sweet scent of rain lingered just beyond her window, intertwining with the earthy fragrance of her garden, an aromatic promise of the moisture to come.

Jasmine remained blissfully unaware that this sudden storm, crackling with energy and cloaked in ominous clouds, was not just a weather change; it marked the beginning of a profound transformation in her life—one whose significance she had yet to grasp. As the wind howled outside, she remained ignorant of the unexpected twists and turns that lay ahead, waiting just beyond the veil of the unfolding night.

Chapter 5

Awakening the Ordinary

Days unfolded into a seamless cycle, each melding into the next, marking yet another Monday filled with promises of new beginnings. The familiar sound of her alarm clock blared relentlessly at 5:50 AM, cutting into Jasmine's slumber, nudging her into the rhythms of her morning routine with its constant chimes.

With blurred, sleep-laden eyes, she stumbled into her cozy kitchen, her bare feet grazing the cool tiled floor. The rich, robust aroma of freshly brewed coffee enveloped her like a warm hug, serving as a comforting reminder of the power found in daily rituals.

The soft morning light streamed through the window, illuminating the scattered remains of yesterday's breakfast—a half-eaten bagel and a few stray crumbs, a testament to her hurried pace.

As she moved through her tasks—pouring steaming coffee into her favorite chipped ceramic mug adorned with a whimsical sunflower, carefully lacing up her well-worn, sturdy shoes, and navigating the bustling streets filled with the symphony of familiar faces each corner shop and street vendor became a piece of her intricate mosaic of life.

Every stoplight felt like a moment to breathe, and each honk of a car horn was a reminder of resilience amidst the ebb and flow of city life as Jasmine embraced her journey with a mix of anticipation and worry.

Once bursting with ambition, Jasmine found herself awakening to the potential of her present, recognizing the unexpected opportunities that lay in embracing the familiar. Each time she turned the key in her apartment door.

Beneath her surface optimism, frustration simmered, signaling a call to action as she faced the absurdity of her situation—an endless loop of predictability that felt stifling. The anticipation of the upcoming weekend, which had shifted from a much-needed break into a motivation for change, turned each tick of the clock into a chance to grab the moment. The vibrancy of life she had once celebrated began to resonate again, rekindled by her courage to seek a transformation that she deeply craved.

Determined to break free from the tiresome cycle that had trapped her, Jasmine committed to charting her days in a worn notebook with frayed edges, capturing even the smallest details the fleeting thoughts that fluttered through her mind during quiet moments, the laughter of friends on a rare night out, and the stark realities of her daily grind to uncover insights that could guide her path forward. The act of writing became a powerful outlet for her emotions, the ink on the paper morphing her frustration into clarity and an invigorating sense of hope.

This journey, while loaded with challenges, sparked a hint of motivation within her. Armed with her notebook and tireless curiosity, she set out to understand the essence of her journey—documenting her highs and lows in meticulous detail. With each entry, she began to reclaim the excitement and spontaneity that once defined her life, resolute in her quest to navigate beyond the fog and embrace the vibrant world that awaited her just outside her door.

Chapter 6

Finding Clarity in the Chaos

Monday had rolled around once again, and Jasmine found herself questioning whether it was genuinely Monday or just another repeat of the same day she had been living for the past month. "Okay, Jasmine, you are the master detective in your own life; it's time to uncover the mystery of why this constant stream of Mondays has settled in and how to break free from it," she mused. The relentless cycle was beginning to wear her down.

As she navigated the same constant tasks of that Monday, she noticed a striking new face among the usual patrons. A man with an incredibly perfect smile approached the counter, a smile that seemed to light up the room. "Oh, who is this and why have I never noticed him before?" she wondered, her heart racing.

The man stepped forward and confidently ordered a mango iced drink, his deep, soothing voice breaking through Jasmine's wondering thoughts.

Just as he was about to pay, he surprised her by asking for her number. Caught off guard, she felt a rush of warmth to her cheeks. She smiled coyly and exchanged playful banter with him, her nerves momentarily forgotten. But despite her fluttering heart, she didn't give him her number.

"He's handsome and sexy," she thought, captivated by the way his smile revealed a charming dimple next to his eye. But as quickly as the thought entered her mind, she shook it away, feeling the familiar weight of self-doubt set in.

She glanced at her friend Sarah, who stood nearby, ready to witness her reaction. "He would never be interested in someone like me, so why even bother?" Jasmine murmured, her voice laced with insecurity.

Sarah, taken aback by Jasmine's comment, shot back with surprising intensity, "If you don't try, you'll never know what could happen! Besides, if he wasn't interested, he wouldn't have asked for your number in the first place!"

"He was just being polite," Jasmine asserted, tucking her hair behind her ear nervously, feeling a mix of embarrassment and frustration. She began to walk away, her thoughts racing.

"Come on, Jasmine! You're amazing!" Sarah called after her, stepping forward to make her point. "You've got so much to offer. You're smart, funny, and genuinely kind. Anyone would be lucky to have you in their life!"

"What if he just wants someone fun and carefree, Sarah? I mean, look at me—I'm just a barista with a knack for awkward conversations and the ability to mentally narrate my daily life. Not exactly exciting," Jasmine replied, trying to deflect Sarah's compliments.

"Sure, every first conversation has its awkward moments! That's part of what makes it exciting! I mean, c'mon—did you see that dimple? How can you resist that?" Sarah teased, nudging her playfully.

Jasmine let out a laugh, the tension easing just a bit. "Okay, maybe he was cute, but what do I do now? Just give him my number and hope for the best?"

"Exactly! If he texts you, just be yourself. It's not like a job interview; it's just a way to connect and have fun!" Sarah encouraged, her eyes sparkling with enthusiasm. "What could possibly go wrong?"

With a soft sigh, Jasmine contemplated the worst-case scenarios. "I could be embarrassed. Or worse, what if he thinks I'm just… weird?"

"Seriously? Every first conversation is a little weird! That's the charm of meeting someone new. And, trust me, you've got plenty of charm to spare," Sarah replied with an encouraging grin.

Jasmine considered her friend's words, finally feeling a flicker of determination. "Alright, you're right. I'll think about it. But if this goes south, you're treating me to ice cream."

"Deal!" Sarah beamed, excitement radiating from her. "Now go get him, detective! This could be the start of something great!"

Jasmine returned to her duties, a newfound bravery settling in her chest as she replayed the encounter in her mind, her heart fluttering with possibility. Jasmine stood at the counter, still replaying the moment in her mind. Sarah watched her, concerned.

"Jasmine, come on. You can't just dismiss him like that," Sarah insisted, leaning against the counter.

"I don't know, Sarah. He's probably just looking for someone fun and carefree. I'm… well, I'm just me," Jasmine replied.

"But you're amazing! You're smart, funny, and kind. Anyone would be lucky to have your number," Sarah countered, crossing her arms. "Sure, if you like awkward conversations and a girl who secretly narrates her life like she's in a movie," Jasmine joked, trying to lighten the mood. Sarah chuckled. "Hey, your inner monologue is quite entertaining! Plus, I think he found it charming."

Jasmine raised an eyebrow skeptically. "Charm or pity? What if he only asked because he felt sorry for me?"

"That's a stretch, even for you. Look, if he didn't find you interesting, he wouldn't have asked for your number in the first place. And he didn't look sorry when he was talking to you," Sarah said with a grin.

"Just think about it? Come on! At least give him a chance!" Sarah replied, nudging her playfully.

"Alright, alright! I'll consider it. But if he turns out to be a total dud, you're buying me ice cream," Jasmine laughed.

Chapter 7

A Journey of Self-Discovery

Today felt remarkably different, as if the world had shifted slightly on its axis. A strange yet familiar sensation lingered in the air, resembling the fragrance of a long-forgotten memory, though she couldn't quite pinpoint its origin.

It was still Monday, and the morning sun filtered gently through the sheer curtains, casting delicate lace-like patterns on the polished hardwood floor. Despite the enchanting scene, a constant throb of a migraine pulsed behind her temples, a reminder of her ongoing battle with discomfort that had become all too familiar.

Determined to change her course, she vowed to herself that no matter how enticing the bubbles of prosecco might seem, she would never indulge again.

After enduring two long months haunted by migraines that blurred the edges of her reality, anyone in her position would reconsider their choices, especially when the simplest pleasures turned into potent reminders of her limitations.

When she arrived at work, a wave of unexpected lightness washed over her, giving her a deep desire to embrace the day fully. The air felt charged with possibilities, and she wondered if this could be the day she finally shook off the gloom that had settled in her heart.

Yet, as her newfound resolve took root, it wavered abruptly when Mrs. Smith entered the café, her demeanor as serious and unyielding as ever. The older woman approached the counter with purposeful strides, ready to order her latest peculiar concoction.

She took on the task of preparing the drink with renewed enthusiasm, her hands moving deftly as she measured the ingredients with precision. Despite their past conversations remaining consistent, this time her responses carried a brightness. "Come on, Jasmine," she urged herself, "don't let anything rattle you!

Focus on bringing a bit of joy to our customers today!" With excitement bubbling inside her like the foam of a freshly poured latte, she was poised to infuse the day with warmth and positivity.

Just then, the mysterious man stepped through the door, reappearing like an enigmatic character from a well-loved novel, creating an overwhelming sense of déjà vu.

He stood confidently at the counter, exuding an air of self-assuredness that was impossible to ignore. With a charming smile that seemed to brighten the room, he asked for two things: her phone number and a mango cooler. Recognition surged through her like a warm tide, accompanied by a flutter of uncertainty in her stomach.

She hesitated for a fleeting moment, weighing the prospect of sharing her number with him—a choice that felt both thrilling and terrifying. Intrigued by the undeniable spark lingering in the air between them, a sweet tension enveloped her, leaving her both nervous and exhilarated, as if she stood on the precipice of an unexpected adventure.

Chapter 8

Uncovering New Beginnings

As she stood at the polished wooden counter of the bustling café, her heart raced at the sight of him entering through the glass door. He walked in with that familiar, warm smile that always sent a delightful flutter through her stomach. The aroma of freshly brewed coffee intertwined with the sweet scent of pastries filled the air, but in that moment, it felt as if the café's soft chatter and the clinking of cups faded into the background.

Time seemed to suspend for a heartbeat, allowing her to focus solely on him—tall and confident, his golden blonde tousled hair catching the soft morning light filtering through the windows. He locked eyes with her, and for a fleeting moment, the chaotic world around them ceased to exist.

"Hey there," he said, approaching her with a casual grace. "You seem different today. Is it a good different?"

She let out a light, genuine laugh that felt freeing. "I think it is! I'm just trying to see things from a new perspective. How about you?"

He leaned comfortably against her desk, his posture relaxed but attentive, his eyes sparkling with a blend of curiosity and mischief. "Same old, same old, but... maybe a little inspired. You know, I really appreciate our conversations. They make my day feel brighter."

Caught off guard by the warmth of his compliment, she felt her cheeks flush a delicate pink. "I feel the same way," she admitted, brushing a stray hair behind her ear, glad to share this moment of vulnerability. "It's nice to have someone to talk to."

He hesitated for a moment, a playful smirk creeping onto his face as he took a step closer. "So, what's the secret to your newfound happiness?"

She shrugged, pretending to ponder the question, her smile teasing at the corners of her lips. "Maybe it's just the fact that I'm learning to enjoy one day at a time. And you... you definitely play a part in that!"

"Me? Really?" he asked, feigning surprise, raising an eyebrow and drawing her into the playful banter. "I didn't know I had that kind of impact!"

"Absolutely! Talking to you always makes me smile. I guess you could say you're my little ray of sunshine," she replied, her voice softening, filled with sincerity.

His expression shifted, softening with a hint of gratitude. "Well, you're definitely my bright spot at work too. I was really hoping to get your number so we could chat outside of the office. Maybe grab coffee sometime?"

A flutter of excitement raced through her, "I'd like that," she said, her heart pounding as she quickly jotted down her number on a piece of lined paper, her handwriting neat and careful.

He took the note with a broad grin, his eyes gleaming with anticipation. "Perfect! I'll text you later, then."

"Sounds good! I'll look forward to it," she replied, unable to suppress the smile that spread across her face, a mix of happiness and anxiety swirling within her. "Awesome! Have a great day," he said, giving her a playful wave as he strolled away, leaving her feeling lighter than before, as if she were walking on air. The world outside felt a little brighter, mixed with the promise of what might come next.

Chapter 9 The Spark of Change

As she felt things starting to go her way, Jasmine decided to head into work with her hair styled a little differently and wearing more makeup. She hoped that her strange but gorgeous crush would be more attracted to her.

Sarah and Tom were going about their day as usual when Jasmine walked through the door. They didn't notice her until she spoke, and then the familiar cycle began again. She served Mrs. Smith and waited for her Mr. Darcy, but nothing happened. Jasmine wondered if maybe the clocks had stopped or if she was coming on too strong. Noticing Jasmine's change in demeanor, Sarah encouraged her to talk about what was going on.

"Oh, Sarah, what if I told you that I've been reliving the same day over and over again for the last three months?" Sarah stared at Jasmine and replied, "Well, we all feel like that. It's called work." Jasmine felt frustrated. "No, Sarah, it's bigger than that. Have you not noticed how my mood started to change last month when Mr. Handsome walked through the door?"

Sarah got up, shook her head, and exclaimed, "My God, you have it bad."

Just then, he walked through the door. Jasmine was overwhelmed with so many emotions, mostly due to Sarah not understanding her. She managed to step out from behind the counter to talk to him away from prying ears.

As Jasmine approached Mr. Handsome, her heart raced with a mix of excitement and anxiety. He was casually perusing the selection of pastries displayed behind the glass.

"Hey there," she greeted him, trying to sound casual despite the butterflies in her stomach. "What can I get for you today?"

He turned, a warm smile spreading across his face. "I think I'll go for that blueberry muffin. It looks fantastic." His rich voice exuded an easy confidence that made Jasmine's heart flutter.

"Good choice! It's one of our best sellers," she said with a bright smile, feeling a rush of excitement. "Do you come here often? I feel like I haven't seen you in a while."

Mr. Handsome chuckled softly, leaning against the counter. "I've been a bit busy, but I always enjoy stopping by when I can. The coffee here is too good to resist, and the barista isn't bad either."

Jasmine felt a connection starting to form between them. "I look forward to it every morning. It helps me survive the monotony of work," she added with a light laugh, hoping to draw him into a deeper conversation.

"Monotony?" he asked, raising an eyebrow. "What do you do?"

"I work here, obviously," she said playfully, gesturing around the café. "I'm also a college student, so juggling both is a bit of a challenge, but I manage."

"That sounds tough," he said, his tone laced with genuine concern. "What are you studying?"

"Psychology," Jasmine replied, starting to feel more at ease. "I've always been fascinated by how people think and behave. What about you? What keeps you busy?"

"I'm in graphic design," he said, his eyes lighting up. "I love creating visual concepts. It's amazing to see an idea come to life on-screen. But sometimes it feels like I'm stuck in the same loop, you know?"

Jasmine's heart skipped a beat. "Oh, I definitely know what you mean; I feel like I've been stuck in this repetitive cycle for months." She hesitated for a moment, contemplating whether to share her secret. "It's like I'm reliving the same day over and over again."

He looked intrigued. "Really? That sounds like it could be either a blessing or a curse. What do you mean?"

She shifted slightly, lowering her voice as if sharing a secret. "It's like I experience the same moments and the same conversations. It's exhausting, and I keep hoping for something to change—something exciting."

Mr. Handsome leaned in, captivated. "What if you took a leap? Change something small and see how that affects your day. You'd be surprised how a little change can make a difference."

Jasmine looked into his eyes, feeling a spark of inspiration. "Maybe you're right. Sometimes it just takes a new perspective or a bit of courage to break the cycle."

He smiled encouragingly. "Exactly! You have to make your own adventure. Besides, the world is too big to stay stuck in one place."

Jasmine felt empowered by his words. "Thanks, I really needed to hear that," she said, her voice more confident now. "And by the way, good luck with your graphic design projects. I bet they're amazing."

He chuckled, clearly flattered. "And good luck with your psychology studies. I'm sure you'll figure out how to break free from your routine soon enough."

As he paid for his muffin, Jasmine couldn't help but feel that this brief encounter held the promise of something new. As he turned to leave, she called out, "I hope to see you again soon!"

"I'll definitely be back," he replied, glancing over his shoulder with a charming smile that made her heart race. "Maybe next time, we can chat over coffee."

With that, he walked out the door, leaving Jasmine with a renewed sense of hope and determination. She returned to the counter, where Sarah watched her intently with a knowing smile on her face.

"Well?" Sarah asked, eager to hear the details.

Chapter 10

Breaking the Cycle

When she finally woke up, a gentle light seeped through her curtains, yet the sun, which she had grown so accustomed to, seemed dimmer than usual. Still in the grasp of sleep, she reached for her phone; a surge of hope flowed through her as she felt the familiar urge to check the date.

To her astonishment, it was Tuesday—Finally! A wave of relief washed over her, lifting the weight from her shoulders like the morning fog dissipating under the sun's gaze. Though she couldn't quite pinpoint what had sparked this sudden shift in her mood, her instincts whispered that the mysterious man she had encountered held the key to her newfound clarity and purpose.

As she moved through the motions of her morning routine, the familiar rituals felt surprisingly more comforting than ever. Brushing her hair felt like a simple act of self-care, savoring the rich aroma of freshly brewed coffee was almost meditative, and toasting whole-grain bread took on a new significance, each moment whispering promises of the day ahead.

The thought of encountering Mrs. Smith, with her sharp tongue and relentless critiques, normally a source of dread, now brought a lighthearted smile to her face. The repetitive nature of her job had often felt stifling, filled with meaningless conversations that faded into the background noise of her life.

Customers would often approach her with random requests that felt devoid of any real connection. However, today was different. With the sun beaming brightly outside, illuminating her small kitchen, and the nagging migraine that had haunted her for days now gone, she felt an enthusiasm bubbling up within her—an energy that seemed to have long faded, now reignited.

As she continued through her morning, a sense of eager anticipation blossomed within her heart. She couldn't shake the thought of potentially meeting the enigmatic man again. His presence had been magnetic, marked by captivating stories and a thoughtful gaze that seemed to peer deep into the recesses of her soul. Each encounter with him intrigued her more than she cared to admit, unraveling pieces of herself she hadn't recognized in ages.

She imagined their upcoming coffee date at the quaint café adorned with a turquoise awning, a whimsical spot that seemed to exude charm and warmth. The thought of sitting across from him, their conversation flowing effortlessly, sent flutters of excitement racing through her. She envisioned uncovering his world, with each story he shared revealing another layer of his complex personality and unique experiences.

Today felt like the start of something profoundly new and beautiful, a promising adventure waiting just around the corner. For the first time in what felt like an eternity, she was ready to embrace it all with open arms and a hopeful heart, eager to see where it might lead her. The past held no reign over her present, for she had chosen to step boldly into the unfolding narrative of her life, and she longed to make each moment count.

Chapter 11 Awakening to Possibility

As usual, Jasmine stirred awake to the jarring sound of her alarm clock blaring at 5:50 AM. However, this morning, she found herself less annoyed by the early hour, even though she would have relished a few more minutes of peaceful slumber. "Is a 7:30 AM wake-up too much to ask for?" she chuckled to herself, the sound echoing softly in her serene bathroom as she prepared for her morning ritual in the shower.

Once she slid into her car, the hum of the engine resonated with her thoughts about the enigmatic man who had unexpectedly woven himself into the fabric of her emotions. "What is his name?" she pondered, determination lacing her voice as she whispered, "If I accomplish nothing else today, I'm going to uncover his identity."

Arriving at work, she greeted Sarah and Tom with the same friendly banter that accompanied their daily routines, yet today felt different. There was a sense of optimism stretching through the café's windows, casting warm shadows on the familiar faces that entered. Among these regulars was Mrs. Smith, whose demeanor often cloaked her like a heavy shroud. She frequently exuded an air of entitlement, demanding utmost respect from the baristas and expecting them to cater to her every whim.

This morning, as Jasmine focused on crafting the perfect cup of coffee for Mrs. Smith, a sudden complaint pierced the atmosphere, accusing the barista of using the wrong milk. Turning around with a beaming smile, Jasmine replied, "Mrs. Smith, I completely understand your frustration, and I'm here to make things right. How about I check our CCTV to verify the order?" Sarah, standing beside her, gasped, her eyes wide with disbelief at Jasmine's unexpected response.

Ignoring Sarah's disbelieving look, Jasmine patiently awaited Mrs. Smith's reaction.

Mrs. Smith, taken aback by this bold offer, had not anticipated pushback. "Um, yes please, I would like to see you check the camera and prove to me that you messed up my order." Jasmine was confident she had not mixed up the milk; she had meticulously prepared that drink day after day, knowing the order by heart.

With purpose, Jasmine made her way to the back of the shop, her heels clicking against the floor. She downloaded the relevant footage onto her work phone, ready to present irrefutable evidence. When she returned, she gently pulled Mrs. Smith aside to share the video.

As they watched the playback together, Mrs. Smith's posture shifted, and a flicker of vulnerability emerged. She unexpectedly revealed to Jasmine the heart-wrenching news of her husband's passing five months prior.

The grief had clung to her, casting a shadow over her daily life; he would always come to the coffee shop each morning, surprising her with various flavored drinks and guaranteed oat milk. She just wanted to keep that alive.

Meeting Mrs. Smith's gaze, Jasmine offered warmth and empathy despite their rocky history. "Grief is a peculiar thing; it can manifest in ways we least expect, but reaching out to others might lighten your burden," she reassured her. To Jasmine's surprise, Mrs. Smith stood there, eyes glistening with unshed tears, acknowledging the truth in her words.

Jasmine found herself wrapping her arms around Mrs. Smith in a comforting hug, feeling the tension melt away.

In that moment of connection, she didn't notice her mysterious man entering the café. He leaned casually against a pillar, a bright smile illuminating his face as he observed the remarkable exchange between Jasmine and Mrs. Smith. After Mrs. Smith took her seat, a familiar warmth blossomed in Jasmine's chest as she turned to him, her heart fluttering in anticipation.

"What a lovely surprise! I never quite know when you'll walk through those doors, but it always brightens my day when you do!" she exclaimed, hovering for a moment, torn between the need to return to her duties and the magnetic pull he had on her.

The tension hung in the air, but he broke it with a playful chuckle. "Well, I do like to keep you on your toes," he said with a twinkle in his eye. "I thought I'd drop by to see if you'd like to join me tonight around 7 PM."

Her face lit up with a sweet smile, one she could hardly contain, and she simply nodded, words eluding her. He returned her smile, and as he turned to leave, he added, "You have my number; text me your address, and I'll pick you up."

A radiant smile lingered on Jasmine's face, infectious in its brightness, drawing Sarah and Tom into her joy as they shared laughter. It was a beautiful sight to witness Jasmine embracing this new chapter in her life. For Sarah and Tom, the transformation felt sudden, yet Jasmine knew it had been a gradual evolution over several months, filling her with warmth and a sense of newfound hope.

As Jasmine stood there, her heart still dancing with excitement from the unexpected invitation, she realized she couldn't let the moment slip away without expressing her curiosity. She called out to him before he could leave.

"Okay, I'll send my address over shortly. I really should know your name," she called after him. "It's Alex." He relyed as he was halfway through the door.

Chapter 12

A Glimpse of Tomorrow

Jasmine wrapped up her workday, and as the clock chimed five o'clock, signaling that it was finally time to leave, her heart raced with a mix of excitement and nerves about the evening ahead. She felt a flutter in her stomach as she practically dashed to her car, the refreshing cool of the evening air filling her lungs and invigorating her spirit as she envisioned the possibilities that awaited her.

Upon arriving home, she burst through the door, her pulse quickening with anticipation. The first stop was her wardrobe, where she meticulously sifted through her carefully curated collection of dresses. Each piece had its own story, but today she was in search of the one that would make her feel truly confident and alluring.

After what felt like an eternity of searching through vibrant colors and elegant fabrics, she finally discovered her crowning jewel: a striking black gown that featured elegant spaghetti straps and a sleek silhouette. The fabric glimmered subtly under the warm light of her bedroom, catching the eye like a starry night. The dress hugged her figure perfectly, while the daring thigh-high slit added a touch of boldness that made her feel empowered. With a wide grin stretching across her face, she couldn't help but shout, "YES, this is the one!"

After indulging in a refreshing shower, she took her time with her makeup, transforming her routine into a ritual. She carefully applied a luminous foundation that highlighted her high cheekbones and created a flawless canvas for her features. Then, she expertly crafted a smoky eye with deep browns and shimmering grays that added depth and mystery to her gaze. As she slipped into her dress, the cool fabric felt luxurious against her skin, a perfect complement to her electrifying mood. She paired the gown flawlessly with her favorite black heels—classic, strappy, and modern—elevating her look in both height and sophistication.

Standing before the mirror, she pondered her hairstyle—should she sweep her hair up into an elegant updo to reveal her graceful neckline, or let it cascade down her shoulders in soft waves? She deliberated, her fingers nervously playing with the loose strands as she weighed her options.

Eventually, she decided on a compromise: leaving her hair down in soft, romantic curls that framed her face beautifully, while pinning one side back with a delicate silver clip that added just enough flair without overshadowing her features.

With every detail perfectly in place, Jasmine felt a surge of confidence wash over her. She could hardly wait for her evening rendezvous with Alex—a thought that made her heart flutter with anticipation. There was an undeniable chemistry between them that excited her, and tonight, she was determined to leave a lasting impression that he wouldn't soon forget.

As she glanced at the wall clock, she noted that it was 6:45 PM. Alex had mentioned he would be picking her up soon, but since she had no idea where he was taking her, her excitement turned into a torrent of restless energy. She settled onto the plush sofa, trying to calm her racing heart and keep herself distracted for the next 15 minutes.

The seconds ticked by slowly, and it was a struggle to focus on anything other than her buzzing anticipation as she kept glancing at the door, eagerly awaiting the sound of the doorbell that would signal the beginning of a night filled with promise.

Chapter 13

<u>The Unknown</u>

Just as Jasmine stole another glance at the clock, the doorbell rang, sending a jolt of excitement coursing through her veins. She took a deep breath, smoothed down her fitted dress, and ran her fingers through her hair to ensure every strand was perfectly in place before gliding to the door.

When she opened it, she was greeted by Alex's warm and inviting smile, which instantly dispelled her nerves. He looked sharp in a crisp white shirt that accentuated his broad shoulders and tailored pants that showcased his impeccable style. His gaze traveled over her, and he let out a breathless, "Wow, you look stunning." The sincerity in his eyes made her blush.

"Thank you! You look fantastic too," Jasmine replied, feeling her initial apprehension fade away. After exchanging a few more heartfelt compliments, they stepped out into the evening air and walked over to Alex's car, where he opened the door for her. She effortlessly got in without revealing too much as she sat down.

As they drove, Alex shared mysterious snippets about the surprise he had planned. Jasmine hung onto his every word, intrigued by his playful hints. The streetlights flickered, casting a soft glow that illuminated the space between them, and she couldn't shake the fluttering feeling in her chest.

Before long, they arrived at a chic rooftop restaurant boasting breathtaking panoramic views of the sparkling city. Jasmine gasped—this was the kind of elegant venue she had only dreamed of visiting.

They were escorted to a beautifully set table with flickering candles that cast a warm light. The ambiance was cozy yet alive with the soft hum of conversation. She could hear the gentle sounds of a piano in the corner of the restaurant playing some jazz song she had never heard before, but she really liked it.

As they chatted over dinner, there was much banter between them. Jasmine sensed herself melting into the moment. She had never felt this way before; the connection between them seemed to grow easier with every laugh and shared story.

The conversation flowed effortlessly, drifting from lighthearted teasing to deeper topics, and she found herself completely engrossed in their discussion.

When dessert arrived—a flawlessly crafted cheesecake drizzled with raspberry coulis—Jasmine couldn't help but feel a swell of gratitude for this unforgettable evening. The food was delicious, but the company was even better. "If that's possible," she thought to herself.

With each passing moment, she realized that tonight was becoming everything she had dreamed of and more.

Feeling brave, she leaned in slightly closer. "So, what's the best surprise you have planned for later?" she teased, playfully raising an eyebrow. Alex paused, a mischievous smile dancing on his lips, and replied, "You'll just have to wait and see." In response, she sat back with a faux sulky expression, enjoying the playful banter. However, Alex, unsure how to navigate this side of her personality, looked at her with a hint of concern. "Honestly, Jaz, I promise you're really going to enjoy it."

She dropped the pretense and came alive with a sultry, "Okay," her smile returning.

The air was thick with anticipation, and as they savored the final bites of their meal, Jasmine knew that whatever lay ahead would only add to the already amazing evening.Just as Jasmine stole another glance at the clock, the doorbell rang, sending a jolt of excitement coursing through her veins. She took a deep breath, smoothed down her fitted dress, and ran her fingers through her hair to ensure every strand was perfectly in place before gliding to the door.

When she opened it, she was greeted by Alex's warm and inviting smile, which instantly dispelled her nerves. He looked sharp in a crisp white shirt that accentuated his broad shoulders and tailored pants that showcased his impeccable style. His gaze traveled over her, and he let out a breathless, "Wow, you look stunning." The sincerity in his eyes made her blush.

"Thank you! You look fantastic too," Jasmine replied, feeling her initial apprehension fade away. After exchanging a few more heartfelt compliments, they stepped out into the evening air and walked over to Alex's car, where he opened the door for her. She effortlessly got in without revealing too much as she sat down.

As they drove, Alex shared mysterious snippets about the surprise he had planned. Jasmine hung onto his every word, intrigued by his playful hints. The streetlights flickered, casting a soft glow that illuminated the space between them, and she couldn't shake the fluttering feeling in her chest.

Before long, they arrived at a chic rooftop restaurant boasting breathtaking panoramic views of the sparkling city. Jasmine gasped—this was the kind of elegant venue she had only dreamed of visiting.

They were escorted to a beautifully set table with flickering candles that cast a warm light. The ambiance was cozy yet alive with the soft hum of conversation. She could hear the gentle sounds of a piano in the corner of the restaurant playing some jazz song she had never heard before, but she really liked it.

As they chatted over dinner, there was much banter between them. Jasmine sensed herself melting into the moment. She had never felt this way before; the connection between them seemed to grow easier with every laugh and shared story.

The conversation flowed effortlessly, drifting from lighthearted teasing to deeper topics, and she found herself completely engrossed in their discussion.

When dessert arrived—a flawlessly crafted cheesecake drizzled with raspberry coulis—Jasmine couldn't help but feel a swell of gratitude for this unforgettable evening. The food was delicious, but the company was even better. "If that's possible," she thought to herself.

With each passing moment, she realized that tonight was becoming everything she had dreamed of and more.

Feeling brave, she leaned in slightly closer. "So, what's the best surprise you have planned for later?" she teased, playfully raising an eyebrow. Alex paused, a mischievous smile dancing on his lips, and replied, "You'll just have to wait and see." In response, she sat back with a faux sulky expression, enjoying the playful banter. However, Alex, unsure how to navigate this side of her personality, looked at her with a hint of concern. "Honestly, Jaz, I promise you're really going to enjoy it."

She dropped the pretense and came alive with a sultry, "Okay," her smile returning.

The air was thick with anticipation, and as they savored the final bites of their meal, Jasmine knew that whatever lay ahead would only add to the already amazing evening.

Chapter 14

A New Dawn

As Alex settled the check, gazing at Jasmine, he was unaware that she couldn't see him standing at the register. Feeling safe to express her excitement, she began a little dance on her chair. However, Alex caught a glimpse of her and smiled at her innocence.

When they stepped outside, the cool evening air wrapped around them. Jasmine made sure her long, blonde hair wes tucked behind her ear and shivered slightly as the chill reached her face. "What's next?" she asked, her eyes sparkling with curiosity and anticipation.

"Just a short drive to the beach," Alex replied, his smile wide and inviting as he opened the car door for her. As they walked toward his sleek silver aldi, Jasmine slid into the passenger seat, her heart racing with the thrill of uncertainty and excitement.

The drive was filled with lighthearted banter and laughter. They reminisced about everything from their favorite childhood memories—like the time Alex tried to build a treehouse and ended up stuck in a tree—to their deepest dreams for the future, such as traveling the world and pursuing their ambitions.

Before long, they arrived at the beach, and Jasmine gasped at the breathtaking view that unfolded before her. the sun had set but the moonlight was refecting in the water and there was noone else on the beach. they walked over to a seceded part of the beach and set up the blanket.

"Wow, Alex! This is stunning!" she exclaimed. "I never thought to come to the beach at night," she mused, gazing at the cloudless sky with stars sparkling above.

"I used to come here a lot just to think, but I haven't been in a while," he said. Just as Jasmine was about to say something, Alex added, "No, no one came with me. I never wanted anyone with me."

"Oh, Alex, that's sad," she said, concern etched across her face.

"I didn't ask, but I'm glad you told me," she said, a slight smile forming on her lips.

"No, you didn't ask, but your face kind of says the words for you before you speak," he smirked, watching as Jasmine blushed once again, embarrassed.

Jasmine took a sip of the rich, cocoa, savoring the warmth that spread through her body as she snuggled closer to Alex, feeling the comfort of his presence. "So, where do we start? I see so many stars! there all beautiful"

"How about we begin by identifying some constellations?" he suggested, excitement evident in his tone as he pointed toward the bright cluster directly above them. "There's Orion! Can you spot him?"

Jasmine followed his gaze, her excitement bubbling over as a smile spread across her face. "There he is! And over there—could that be the Big Dipper?"

"Exactly!" Alex nodded enthusiastically.

"I see one of the brightest stars has fallen from the sky and landed next to me," his voice was low and alluring. "Oh, Alex, that's so sweet! Did you come up with that yourself or hear it in a movie?" she teased, a playful smile dancing on her lips.

"Not me. I heard it in a film and wanted to say it to someone special. You're worthy of all the lines," he replied, his tone jovial but tinged with a hint of embarrassment.

As she shyly glanced down at her hands, he gently reached out, lifting her chin with his fingers so their gazes met once more. They locked eyes for what felt like an eternity, the stars above fading into the background as the world around them disappeared. Then, in that charged moment, he leaned in and kissed her—a slow, purposeful kiss that left them both breathless when they finally parted.

Jasmine tried to regain her composure, laughter bubbling up as she attempted to steer them back to the awe of stargazing. She cleared her throat and exclaimed, "Alright, that bright one over there is going to be called 'The Dreamer' because it captures all the wishes we'll make tonight!"

Alex turned to her, his eyes sparkling with interest. "The Dreamer, huh? I love it! What other names do you have for our starry friends?"

With each star they discovered, Jasmine spun whimsical tales, her laughter echoing against the tranquil backdrop of the night. Hours flew by as they exchanged secrets and cherished wishes, and with every shared moment, the bond between them grew deeper and stronger. He watched her being aminated with each sentance and it made hiim closer to her.

When the first shooting star streaked across the sky, leaving a golden tail in its wake, Jasmine gasped in delight. "There it is! My wish is to continue having magical moments like this forever."

He smiled, his heart swelling at her hopeful words. "That's a beautiful wish. Mine is that we never lose this sense of adventure and spark."

As they lay together, gazing at the infinite cosmos, they both knew that there were signs of the new morning coming in. they knew this was a good sign of being the begining of their journey together.

Chapter 15

The Turning Point

As they continued to gaze up at the stars, the soft hum of the nighttime surrounded them like a comforting blanket, punctuated only by the occasional rustle of leaves in the gentle breeze. The vast sky, a canvas of shimmering constellations, seemed to stretch on forever. Jasmine nestled closer to Alex, feeling an overwhelming sense of safety and warmth emanating from his strong presence.

"Have you ever thought about what's out there?" she said aloud, her eyes dancing across the various stars, their twinkling lights torching her imagination. "What if there are other worlds just like ours, filled with life and stories waiting to be discovered?"

Alex chuckled softly, the sound rich and inviting, clearly captivated by her adventurous spirit. "I do sometimes. It's fascinating to think that there could be other beings gazing up at their own night skies, pondering the same mysteries we find ourselves caught up in."

Jasmine beamed, inspired by their shared moment of wonder. "Imagine if we could travel between those worlds, meeting new people and sharing their dreams and experiences. That would be absolutely fascinating!"

"Definitely! It would be like living a never-ending adventure," he replied, excitement evident in the spark in his eyes. "We could gather stories and experiences from every corner of the universe, each one adding a new chapter in the story of our lives."

"And then we could share those stories under the stars," she replied dreamily, her voice a soft whisper that harmonized with the night. "Just like this."

For a while, they sat in comfortable silence, allowing the stunning view of the night to wash over them, filling the air with a real sense of possibility. The stars twinkled above, like tiny diamonds scattered across black velvet, as if they were granting their dreams and hopes approval. Jasmine's mind drifted into the realm of future possibilities, and she felt a deep connection to Alex, as well as to everything that lay ahead—an unknown adventure ready to unfold.

"Promise me something," she said suddenly, her voice taking on a serious tone, breaking the tranquil spell.

"Anything," Alex replied, turning to face her fully, his expression softening with curiosity and concern.

"Promise that no matter where life takes us, we'll always find our way back to moments like this. Moments where we can dream and explore together—just like we are now."

"I promise," he said with unwavering sincerity, his voice steady and full of emotion. "No matter what happens, I want to share those magical moments with you."

A wave of warmth rushed through Jasmine at his words, the gravity of their promises wrapping around them tighter than the blanket spread beneath them. As they leaned back against the soft fabric, Jasmine playfully nudged Alex, her eyes sparkling with mischief. "Alright, Mr. Stargazer, what's next on our agenda?"

They remained cozy and content for what felt like an eternity, wrapped in each other's warmth. Suddenly, Alex muttered, "Shit." Jasmine's heart skipped a beat as she looked at him, her alertness piqued. "What?" she asked, with concern across her face.

Alex's expression shifted to one of guilt, his brow slightly furrowed. "It's 5 AM, and you need to be at work soon. I promised I would have you back bright-eyed and bushy tailed." The realization hit them both, and they burst into giggles, the urgency of the moment playfully countered by their shared sense of humor.

"Oh well, looks like I'll be the one opening up the office today," Jasmine said, a cheeky smile spreading across her face. "Maybe the couch in the office will be comfy enough for me to catch a quick nap."

Alex opened his mouth to respond as if he had something to say, but paused, the weight of the moment convincing him that now wasn't the best time to bring anything else up.

They quickly gathered their things, smiles still plastered on their faces as they hurried back to Jasmine's place. Once there, she dashed inside to grab a clean uniform while Alex waited in the car, his heart filled with warmth from the night they had spent together.

After she re-emerged, he dropped her off at work, and the morning light was really coming up over the horizon. With a soft, lingering peck on her cheek, he watched her walk toward the building, their smiles radiating joy—a silent promise shared in that fleeting moment before they parted ways.

Chapter 16

Threads of Change

Jasmine arrived at the store and started up all the cameras and coffee machines. As she worked, she found herself daydreaming about her dream date with her ideal man. She had never believed in love at first sight or even in the early stages of a relationship, but this time felt different. She sensed a strong connection with him, which genuinely surprised her. Her monotonous routine had kept her from anticipating any of this.

After setting up the store, she checked her phone one last time before opening the doors. A message from Alex appeared.

"Thank you for coming with me last night. I really enjoyed myself and wondered if you were free this weekend. My friend is getting married, and I was struggling to find someone to go with, but then I met you, and it made perfect sense that I was waiting for you."

She quickly replied, **"OMG, Alex! That's a surprise. You don't normally get wedding invites until a few months in, but yes, I'll be your date! I would love to."**

Although she could have waited for another message, she needed to focus on work. Just then, Sarah walked in five minutes late. She took one look at Jasmine and teased, "So no 10 PM bedtime, then?" As Sarah grabbed her apron, she giggled so much that Jasmine almost playfully hit her. "We'll talk later, yeah?" Sarah said as she got started on her morning tasks.

As the day went on, Jasmine wanted to pick up her phone and chat with Alex, but he was probably busy with work and just as tired as she was, especially after their late-night/early-morning outing.

When 5 PM rolled around, she practically ran past Sarah and Tom as she dashed out of the coffee shop. Immediately, she checked her phone and found another message from Alex. A huge smile spread across her face.

"I know, but I care far more than I expected, and I really want to show you off. It made me so happy that you said yes."

Jasmine was taken aback but quickly realized she felt the same way. She replied, **"Oh, Alex! I'm so happy you said that. My brain couldn't handle it being one-sided."**

Almost instantly, Alex replied, **"I truly am happy you said yes because now I can surprise you again."**

She wondered what surprise he could have planned; it seemed unusual for him to have a regular day without something special.

"And what is this surprise this time? I think you would struggle to top the last one," she texted, giggling to herself.

"Okay, Jasmine, I'll come out with it. I've booked a room at the hotel where the reception is being held. There are two single beds, but if we wanted to, we could do something else. No pressure or worry if you didn't want to."

Jasmine sat in her car, mouth agape in shock at his last text. She didn't know how to respond. She thought, "Yes, he is gorgeous and a fantastic kisser. But do I want to take that step so soon after just one date?"

Chapter 17

Awakening to Hope

It was Friday, and after weeks of juggling demanding long Mondays at work, Jasmine finally managed to secure a last-minute day off in anticipation of the wedding she had been eagerly awaiting tomorrow. Excitement surged through her, mingled with a hint of nerves; she hadn't seen Alex for a couple of days, yet their late-night phone calls, filled with laughter, shared dreams, and plans for the future, had kept their connection vibrant and steady.

Determined to make the most of this rare free time, she set her alarm for 9 a.m., relishing the thought of sleeping in — a true extravagance since her last weekend off had been months ago. When she awoke, the soft morning sunlight poured through her bedroom window, casting gentle patterns on the walls. A warm smile spread across her face as she reflected on how far their relationship had come and how much they had to look forward to.

Slowly, she climbed out of bed, making her way down the familiar staircase, taking a moment to appreciate each step beneath her feet. In the kitchen, she prepared her usual cup of rich, aromatic coffee, watching as the dark liquid danced in the pot and filled the air with its warm, scent that signaled the start of her day. This morning ritual, a cherished moment of serenity, allowed her to pause before the day unfolded.

With her warm mug cradled in her hands, Jasmine stepped out into the garden, where the fresh morning air carried the gentle fragrance of blooming Roses and Lavender. The petals swayed in the soft breeze, creating a calming rhythm.

As she glanced around, savoring the peaceful beauty of her surroundings and the cheerful songs of birds returning from their winter migration, she thought, "I don't remember ever seeing the garden at this hour before." The stillness enveloped her, connecting her deeply to nature and her surroundings.

Suddenly, the piercing sound of a car alarm shattered her calm, jolting her back into reality. Laughing at her own jumpiness, she shook her head lightly, reminding herself to stay focused. "Okay, Jasmine, your task for today is to find something special that will make Alex love you even more," she said aloud, her voice filled with determination and a hint of excitement. She brainstormed the possibilities: a thoughtful gift, a heartfelt handwritten note, or perhaps something simple yet meaningful that spoke to their shared memories and experiences.

With a renewed sense of purpose energizing her, she turned and headed back upstairs. She paused in front of the mirror, smoothing her hair and adjusting her clothes—the fabric draping comfortably, a reflection of her anticipation for the day ahead. After gathering her purse, she made a mental list of the stores she wanted to visit, her mind racing with ideas on how to make this wedding unforgettable—not only for them but for everyone involved.

As she navigated through the shops in the bustling city center, she found herself straying from her original list, her curiosity leading her. Stepping confidently into Marks & Spencer, she headed straight for the lingerie department, her heart racing as she searched for something that would truly knock Alex's socks off. A sly smile crept across her face as she contemplated the excitement this might bring.

Her eyes landed on a stunning strapless black lace teddy paired with a matching gown. Without hesitating or glancing at the price, she quickly grabbed her size and made a beeline to the counter to pay, feeling an exciting rush knowing this was the missing piece in her collection.

Next, she set out in search of the perfect dress. After what felt like hours of searching, Jasmine stumbled upon a charming little boutique featuring unique, one-off dresses. There, she discovered a gorgeous, crushed velvet red dress that had a silhouette like her black one at home but was undeniably sexier.

After trying it on, she felt an immediate sense of confidence and appeal wash over her, a sly smile forming on her face as she excitedly considered the possibilities for tomorrow's wedding and the special moments that awaited her and Alex.

Chapter 18

A Shift in Perspective

Saturday arrived, and Jasmine felt a whirl of excitement and nerves as she meticulously packed her overnight bag. She furrowed her brow, deeply contemplating each item, and re-packed her belongings three, maybe even four times. Finally, she paused, letting out a soft sigh as she chided herself, "Stop overthinking this."

Glancing at the antique clock on her bedroom wall, she noted the time slipping away; Alex was set to pick her up at 6:00 PM. They needed to check in at the venue and arrive at the reception with plenty of time to spare. With a determined nod to herself, she leaped into the shower, the warm water cascading over her skin and washing away the dust and fatigue from a long day of cleaning—a chore she loathed but recognized was long overdue.

After her shower, she followed her familiar self-care routine: applying a rich moisturizer to her skin and taking her time with a careful shave. With her hair still damp, she expertly set it in curlers, each twist precise, all while contemplating the outfit she had laid out for the evening— a stunning navy-blue dress that hugged her curves just right. Standing before the full-length mirror, she took a deep breath and scrutinized her appearance. Even she had to admit, she looked breathtaking, her confidence shining through.

Once she carefully removed the curlers and ensured her hair was completely dry, she styled it into her signature French roll, meticulously arranging it to frame her face with two artfully loose strands that accentuated her cheekbones.

Just as she applied the final touches of her makeup—a light dusting of shimmering highlighter and a bold swipe of crimson lipstick—the doorbell rang right on cue—Alex had arrived. Jasmine took her time descending the stairs, savoring the moment, absorbed in her anticipation before opening the door.

She didn't say a word at first, choosing instead to gauge his reaction. He didn't disappoint. His eyes widened in appreciation as he took in her appearance, and with a breathy "Hi," he swallowed hard, clearly taken aback by her transformation.

Jasmine smiled coyly and lifted a finger to signal that she needed just a minute. Quickly, she slipped behind the door to don her chic slingback heels and grabbed her overnight bag before stepping outside with an air of confidence, her hips swaying gracefully with each step.

As she glided toward his sleek, silver aldi parked in the driveway, Alex stepped up beside her, his hands finding her waist as he leaned in, his breath warm against her ear. "I see exactly what you're doing, and it's utterly irresistible," he murmured, a hint of mischief dancing in his voice. He pressed closer, their bodies almost melding together, and an intoxicating sigh escaped her lips, igniting an irresistible energy between them as the enchanting evening unfolded ahead.

Chapter 19

A Spark of Joy

As they approached the grand entrance of the hotel, its marble façade gleaming in the afternoon sun, he checked them in with a warm, engaging smile. After receiving the key, he took their bags, expertly maneuvering through the elegant lobby decorated with sparkling chandeliers and vibrant floral arrangements, before heading up the plush carpeted staircase to their meticulously prepared room.

Jasmine followed, her heart racing with a mixture of excitement and disbelief. She slightly tilted her head, captivated by the beauty of the moment, and sighed softly. It still felt surreal to her that this charming guy liked her, and even more impressive was how much she had come to like him in such a short time.

As they reached the reception area, the ambiance buzzed with laughter and lively conversation of wedding guests reveling in the joyous occasion. Alex's eyes sparkled with enthusiasm as he introduced Jasmine to Tim and Jayne, the radiant bride and groom, who were two of his closest friends. "Tim and Jayne, how are you? Congratulations!" he exclaimed, enveloping them in warm, heartfelt hugs. "This is Jasmine, the girl I couldn't stop talking about." The couple exchanged intrigued glances, their smiles widening with curiosity.

"Hi, you two! Congratulations! You both look absolutely stunning," Jasmine said, her voice light and sincere, her gaze flickering between the couple. "Um, but what was that look you shared just now?" she added, her brows furrowing slightly in confusion. Tim and Jayne laughed gently, their eyes twinkling with playful mischief. "Because… Alex here hasn't stopped raving about you for months! We just had to meet the incredible girl he's been talking about," they replied, their words making Jasmine blush a deeper shade of pink.

She was momentarily flattered and mystified, mulling how he had spoken so highly of her over what felt like only a few weeks. She glanced sidelong at Alex and, almost reluctantly, said, "I'll explain shortly." He turned back to Tim and Jayne, wishing them well and expressing his happiness for their day. Did he really have to put me on blast like that? she thought, struggling to suppress a smile. "Anyway, I need to show Jasmine the rest of the place, so I'll love you and leave you for now," he said, nodding as he guided her away.

They wandered through the hotel's scenic gardens, where fragrant flowers swayed gently in the warm breeze, their vibrant colors painting a serene backdrop. As they strolled along the paved walkway dappled with sunlight filtering through the leafy canopy, Alex sensed he needed to clarify the earlier comment. Mustering his courage, he plunged in, "So about that comment…"

"Yeah, what was that all about? We've only known each other for a few weeks, right?" Jasmine asked, her curiosity palpable. She was acutely aware that their connection was more profound, but she wasn't sure whether he comprehended that depth yet.

"Well," he began, his voice taking on a more serious tone, "I was brought in to help you find yourself and break out of this slump you've been in." He cast his eyes downward, feeling the weight of vulnerability, but he pressed on. "I didn't plan on falling for you. I've been observing you for a while—watching you navigate through struggles, even from afar, before we met."

The candidness of his words hung in the air, creating a moment of intimate silence between them. Jasmine's breath caught in her throat, and after a beat, she broke the tension with a teasing chuckle, "Wow, that's a bit creepy." They shared a laugh, the sound echoing lightly in the serene garden, allowing a sense of ease to return.

"I really do want to spend the night with you," Alex started, his voice cautiously hopeful, "but if you don't…" His sentence hung in the air, unfinished, a hint of uncertainty. But before he could complete his thought,

Jasmine playfully raised a finger to his lips, silencing him. "Shushhhhhhh," she murmured, wearing a mischievous smile that sparkled with promise.

As they made their way back to the reception, the atmosphere shifted to one of romance, with soft music playing in the background and couples twirling elegantly on the dance floor. They stepped into this enchanting moment, embracing each other tightly as they began to dance, their hearts beating in sync.

He looked deep into her eyes, capturing her gaze, and leaned in to whisper softly in her ear, "Are you ready?" Her response was a radiant smile that slowly spread across her lips, illuminating her face and igniting a warmth in his heart, signaling that they were both ready to explore what lay ahead.

Chapter 20

Whispers of Desire

Alex and Jasmine found themselves enveloped in the dimly lit ambiance of the Grand Hotel, a haven away from the bustling city outside. The faint hum of conversations, clinking glasses, and the occasional laughter formed a soothing backdrop, complementing the intimate moment they were about to share. The soft glow of the antique chandelier cast a warm light over the elegantly furnished room, filling it with a sense of secret luxury and anticipation.

As they drew closer, their gazes locked with an intensity that ignited an electric spark between them. The air full of unspoken desirers, an invisible thread weaving their souls together, drawing them into an orbit of desire.

Alex, heart pounding in his chest, gently brushed a delicate strand of hair behind Jasmine's ear, his fingertips grazing her soft skin, sending a cascade of shivers tumbling down her spine. It was magic in the air, a moment frozen in time where nothing else mattered but the two of them.

Drawing in a shaky breath, Jasmine stepped nearer, feeling the warmth radiating from Alex, His hands tenderly cradled her face, his touch sending electric waves of warmth through her body. He leaned in, their lips colliding in a soft, uncertain kiss that quickly deepened, each shared breath intensifying the connection as if their very souls were merging.

A soft sigh escaped Jasmine's lips—a sound that spoke of her longing, her desire—as she melted against him, oblivious to the world beyond the hotel room, lost in the magic of the moment.

They surrendered to the intoxicating experience, their hands exploring the warmth of skin beneath the fabric that separated them. Alex's fingers traced a gentle path down Jasmine's back, pulling her even tighter against him, while her own hands wove through his hair, feeling the silkiness of his locks that had long captured her attention. Their kisses grew more urgent, laden with the weight of their emotions, each caress igniting a deep longing neither of them had ever experienced before.

Outside, the world faded into a distant murmur as if the universe itself had conspired to give them this moment, leaving only the two of them wrapped in their own cocoon of passion.

Jasmine's heart raced, the thrill of the encounter igniting every nerve ending, making her feel alive and desired, utterly consumed by the heat enveloping them. With a flutter of excitement blossoming in her chest, she slipped off her dress, standing before him in the elegant black teddy she had chosen just the day before—a flattering ensemble that accentuated her form beautifully.

The way he looked at her then, a mixture of admiration and heightened desire, sent waves of exhilaration coursing through her body, stirring emotions she barely understood.

He pulled her in close once more, kissing her deeply, and their chemistry—undeniable and potent—filled the room like an intoxicating fragrance.

They navigated their way to bed in a playful burst, laughter mingling with soft sighs of delight as they clumsily shed the last remnants of their clothing, feeling free and uninhibited. With each kiss that amplified their connection, warmth and laughter entwined, pulling them onto the plush sheets that welcomed their bodies, creating a place where they could freely explore their desires.

With every brush of his lips along her collarbone, Alex ignited a trail of warmth down her skin, each tender touch sending sparks of pleasure racing through her veins. Jasmine could hardly contain herself; she pressed him closer, their bodies entwining in a beautiful dance of longing and exploration as the boundaries of desire blurred amidst their exploration of each other. Each sigh and gasp echoed a story of its own, filled with passion and discovery born from the magnetic pull between them.

In that luxurious hotel room, surrounded by soft pillows and the exhilarating thrill of the night, they surrendered wholeheartedly to their passion. They created a world of their own—one full of whispered secrets, soft laughter, and fervent kisses that seemed to stretch the night into infinity.

As time slipped away, they crafted memories that would linger long after the stars faded into dawn—a mix of emotion, longing, and the sweet sacrifice of bodies and hearts, leaving them breathless yet fulfilled in their intimate moments.

Chapter 21

Enchanted Moments

The following morning, warm sunlight streamed through the sheer curtains, casting golden patterns on the bed where they lay entwined in each other's arms. They had fallen asleep after a night filled with laughter and intimate whispers, and their hearts were still racing with the echoes of those moments. As they opened their eyes, they exchanged looks filled with undeniable love and tenderness.

Jasmine smiled softly, her mind already drifting to her morning ritual: brewing a fresh pot of coffee. No matter where she found herself, the comforting aroma of coffee was a non-negotiable start to her day. However, Alex, with his mischievous grin, was in a playful mood and wasn't about to let her escape. He playfully straddled her, pinning her down gently but firmly, a twinkle of mischief in his eyes.

"Tell me how you feel," he demanded playfully, clearly enjoying this moment of intimacy and light-heartedness.

Jasmine gazed deep into his eyes, searching the depths of his soul as if unlocking secrets. "Alex, I never knew that someone could change my life as much as you have, and I am forever grateful for that. I love you dearly for this. Last night was such a romantic and sensual surprise; it made me want to give myself completely to you.

I didn't realize that anyone else could truly understand my 'groundhog moments'—those days when I felt stuck in a loop. But I knew I wanted to be intimate with you even before our conversation. Your heartfelt confession last night solidified it for me: you are the one."

A radiant smile blossomed on her face, illuminating the room and her heart. Before he could respond, she teasingly added, "Now let me put the coffee on, or you will see a mean side of me!"

Alex couldn't help but chuckle, relenting as he let her slip out from underneath him. He settled himself on the edge of the bed, watching her with affectionate amusement as she walked to the kitchen, her hair dancing with each step.

When Jasmine returned, coffee in hand and the rich aroma filling the air, she sat next to him on the edge of the bed, her heart racing in anticipation. Without missing a beat, he began to answer the question he had posed to her moments before.

"Jaz," he began, his voice soft and sincere, "I have watched you from afar for a long time. I think, if there is such a thing, I fell in love with you the very first moment I laid eyes on you. I came to you with the intention of being just a friend, but your warm aura and radiant smile drew me in so powerfully that there was simply no way I could ignore my heart's desire."

As he spoke, Jasmine's heart swelled with joy. The sincerity in his words washed over her like a comforting wave. She felt a tear of happiness gather in her eye, almost overwhelming her. She blinked quickly to hold back her emotions, her heart so full it felt as if it might burst.

She was truly elated to hear this from him—someone she had come to care for so deeply. She leaned in and gave him a deep, passionate kiss as a thank you and a hope for the future.

Chapter 22

Timelines of the Heart

As they left the hotel room hand in hand, the soft morning light flooded the hallway, casting a warm glow on their intertwined fingers. They walked past a pair of newlyweds who, with their flushed cheeks and radiant smiles, looked just as smitten as they felt. With a gentle sigh, they checked out of the hotel, and Alex turned to Jasmine, his eyes sparkling with curiosity. "What did you want to do now?" he asked, a hint of mischief in his voice.

Jasmine shook her head, the uncertainty written across her face, each thought flitting away like butterflies. Alex leaned in closer, brushing a strand of hair behind her ear, and planted a soft kiss on her lips. "Did you want to come back to mine? I can make scrambled eggs," he offered playfully.

She chuckled, the sound brightening the mood. "Scrambled eggs, huh? Okay, scrambled eggs it is!"

Once they reached Alex's flat, Jasmine was pleasantly surprised by how immaculate it was. For a bachelor, it was surprisingly tidy, with every item neatly in its place. "Clearly," she mused to herself, "instead of learning to cook, he spends his time keeping this place spotless."

After Alex whipped up the brunch, the rich aroma of eggs and toast wafted through the air, they settled together on the couch, their bodies relaxed but their minds engaged. Their conversation flowed effortlessly, shifting to their dreams and aspirations for the future. Jasmine shared her story, her eyes lighting up as she reminisced about her initial goal of becoming an interior designer. She detailed the setbacks she faced in landing a job in her dream field and how she eventually shifted gears, embracing psychology instead. "I really enjoy it," she confessed, her voice tinged with longing, "but I still wish I could help people create their ideal spaces."

Alex was captivated, hanging onto her every word, fully immersing himself in her aspirations. However, he was so lost in thought that he didn't immediately register Jasmine's question. "What about you? Alex? What did you want to do?" When he finally snapped back to reality, he chuckled awkwardly. "Honestly? Anything but being a salesperson. I know I'm good at it, but my heart's not in it. I just... haven't found my true passion yet." They shared a laugh, their playful banter reinforcing their blossoming connection.

Then, Jasmine dared to tread into the waters, broaching the topic that had lingered in the air between them. "So, Alex, what did you mean yesterday when you said you were sent?" His cheeks flushed with embarrassment, and he shifted uncomfortably on the couch. "It's going to sound strange," he began hesitantly, "but I'm a time traveler. You and I are meant to be together. There are obstacles in the future for us, and I was sent back to help you find yourself again."

She burst into laughter, the sound bubbling up unexpectedly, but when she glimpsed his serious demeanor, her amusement faded. "I'm serious," he insisted, his gaze unwavering. "I've watched you through the window for months. And by months, I mean eight. I kept coming back until it was decided I was the answer to bring you out of your slump."

Jasmine's laughter gave way to disbelief as she processed his words. "So what you said about graffic graphic design and that you loved it—that was all a lie? Just something to say? You know how I feel about you; you're closer to me than anyone I've ever been with, and you throw this at me? That's just... cruel."

Feeling a surge of anger, she turned to leave, but Alex gently grasped her arm and guided her back to sit beside him. "No, Jasmine, it's not a lie. Yes, I'm in sales back in my timeline, and I never wanted to be there, im at collage trying to get back into graphic design. In the meantime, it turns out I'm good at sales" he confessed, vulnerability etched across his features. The knot in Jasmine's stomach began to twist tighter, and instinctively, she shifted closer to him.

"What was the purpose of you coming back to this time to meet me?" she asked, a flicker of hope igniting in her chest. She desperately wanted to hear what he had to say.

"I came back for you," he replied earnestly, his eyes reflecting a deep sincerity. "Even though your motivation had waned in my time, I still loved you. Seeing you in your own timeline only made me fall harder for you. So yes, while I did bend the truth to avoid this conversation last night, I'm glad we're having it now. Do you still want me, Jaz, now that you know the truth?"

Tension hung between them, mingling with an uncertain but hopeful anticipation, as Jasmine contemplated the weight of his words.

She sat there for a few minutes and said I need to think. I'll call you tonight, is that ok?" Alex looked a little low and didn't want her to leave, but he knew she needed this time to accept what he was saying. "ok ill speak to you tonight"

Chapter 23

Unravelling the mystery

Once Jasmine got home, she sat on the couch, staring into space. She was trying to weigh the pros and cons of what had just happened.

- She loves him—a love that seemed to come from nowhere.
- He hasn't been completely truthful.
- He has such a cute smile.
- He's sweet.
- Their connection is undeniable.

Before she listed any more reasons, she thought about the only thing really stopping her: the fact that he left out some of the truth. While that's not okay, he did it for what he believed were the right reasons.

- He clearly loves her; he's been talking about her to his friends.
- He made her believe it was she who was going crazy... well, he couldn't tell her everything.

About 30 minutes later, Jasmine heard a knock at the door, sending a flutter of nerves through her stomach. She took a moment to collect herself, smoothing her hair and adjusting her shirt before opening the door to find Alex standing there, his expression a mix of eagerness and concern.

"Hey," he said softly as he stepped inside, the familiar warmth of his presence filling the room. He looked around, noting the dim lighting and the scattered books and blankets on the couch. "I hope I'm not interrupting anything."

"No, not at all," she replied, her voice steady despite the anxious beating of her heart. "I really wanted to talk." She motioned for him to sit, and after a moment's hesitation, he settled onto the couch beside her.

Silence draped over them, and Jasmine glanced down at her hands, fidgeting with her fingers. "I've been doing a lot of thinking since our last conversation," she began, her voice soft but firm. She paused, searching for the right words to express the whirlwind of feelings inside her.

Alex turned to face her, his eyes serious and attentive. "I'm here for whatever you have decided. Just know I care about you, and I'm ready to be completely honest this time."

She met his gaze, taking a deep breath. "I love you, Alex. But the truth matters to me. I can't be with someone who's not being completely honest, even if you did it out of love or to protect me."

His expression shifted. "I understand," he replied, his voice low. "I didn't mean to make you doubt yourself, and I never wanted to hurt you. There were things I thought I was protecting you from, but I see now that I just made it worse."

As he spoke, Jasmine could see the sincerity in his eyes. The warmth that she had always felt when they were together began to flicker back to life, but she knew they needed to navigate this rocky terrain carefully.

"What was it you didn't tell me?" she asked gently, her heart pounding as she braced herself for his answer. He ran a hand through his hair, clearly grappling with his thoughts.

"I didn't mention that we were married and divorced in my time," he admitted, his voice shaky. "I didn't want you to see me differently. I thought if I told you too soon, it would scare you away."

"So, we were married—how far in the future is this?" Jasmine asked, taking a deep breath. "It's in 2030," Alex replied.

"Five years from now?" she said, shocked. "So, what was it that separated us?"

Alex knew he had to tell her for this chance to work. "You get your motivation back and not falling into depression. I wanted to help you, but you kept pushing me away," he explained, looking down at his hands.

Jasmine felt her heart softening as she lifted his chin to meet her gaze.

The tension in the air began to dissipate, replaced by a flickering hope that they could work through this. Jasmine nodded slowly. "Okay, I'm willing to listen. But this is just the beginning. There will need to be trust, and that won't happen overnight."

"Agreed," Alex replied earnestly. "Let's take it step by step. I'll share everything, and we can figure this out together."

"While I'm being honest with you. I may need to nip in and out of this and my time so i can keep things moving there but I would really love if we could continue this relationship. To be honest its going better this time round already as I knew you before I did in my time and i think the reason it failed is i met you too late the first time."

Jasmine sat down on his knee and kissed him softly and said i would wait for you forever.

Printed in Dunstable, United Kingdom